KT-224-673

Contents

Series Reading Consultant: Prue Goodwin,
Lecturer in literacy and children's books,
University of Reading

Chapter One
Lost Ball

"Go and put the corner flags in, Alex, while I fix the nets up."

"OK, Dad . . ." Alex said, trying to keep the ball off the ground using just his weaker right foot, "three . . . four . . . in a minute . . ."

"Now, Alex. The other lads will be here soon."

"Six . . . ohh—"

Alex lost control and the ball bounced away from him. He gave a little shrug and trudged to the shed to collect the flag posts. It was his usual job once Dad had marked out the pitch with fresh white lines.

He sometimes wondered why nobody else came to help get things ready before Athletic's Sunday League home matches.

"We don't mind, do we, son?" Dad would say. "Beats standing around in the cold, doing nothing."

Alex felt like pointing out
that they wouldn't have to get
to the park so early if they had
nothing to do. He could stay in
his warm bed a bit longer.

He stuck two posts in place
and then set off for the far end
of the pitch. He dribbled the
ball along, head down, doing a
running commentary:

"... and here's young Alex Jelley on the wing — he beats one man, beats another — they can't stop him ..."

The ball was suddenly whipped away off his toes.

"That's stopped you!" laughed Louis. "You should look where you're going, Jelly-Belly."

Alex pulled a face. He didn't like people making fun of his name – and his shape.

"Can I have my ball back?" he asked.

"You'll have to get it off us first," Ben grinned, swapping passes with Louis.

Alex didn't bother. He knew he didn't stand a chance. They were the team's best players. *He* was lucky even to get picked as one of the subs.

"Hey! Smart ball, this," Louis cried, flicking it up into his hands for a closer look. "We could use it in the match."

"Come on, Alex, hurry up!"
Dad called out. "You can have
a kickabout with your mates
when you've got all those posts
set up."

"Yeah, get on with it, Jelly-
Belly," Louis chuckled. "Just
leave the ball with us."

Chapter Two
Unlucky?

"Here's your chance, son," said
Dad, tossing Alex a faded
green shirt. "The manager's
picked you as one of the subs."

Alex caught the shirt and
wasn't surprised to see the

number thirteen on the back.
He wondered if it was the
manager's little joke. He'd only
played twice for Athletic and
both times he'd had this same
shirt.

"Unlucky for some," he heard
Ben snigger from the corner of
the changing hut.

"Yeah, unlucky for us, if Jelly-Belly has to come on," muttered Louis. "He's only in the squad because his dad does all the work for the club."

Alex ignored them and tugged the shirt over his head. It seemed to have shrunk in the wash since last time he'd worn it. It was even more of a tight fit than before and there was now a hole under one of the arms.

As the players left the hut, Alex found the other substitute, Rafiq, by his side. "Looks like you've lost that new ball of yours," said Rafiq, seeing the manager toss it to the referee. "I thought it was a birthday present."

"Yes, it was, but Louis wanted to play with it."

Rafiq nodded in sympathy. He knew full well that what Louis wanted, Louis got. Louis was the team captain – and his dad was the manager.

"Watch the game, son," said Alex's dad, taking up his usual position on the touchline with a flag. "You never know when we might need you to come on."

Alex guessed that it would
not be very soon, if at all.
When the match kicked off, he
and Rafiq began practising
together away from the pitch
with a spare ball.

"You go in goal and I'll take shots at you," said Rafiq.

Alex went to stand between a couple of trees near the hut. "Score three goals and then we swap places."

"OK," Rafiq agreed. "Just as long as you don't let any in on purpose."

Alex grinned. "As if I would!" And he didn't.

Rafiq beat him with his second effort, but it must have taken him at least another ten goes before he managed to score again.

Rafiq collapsed to the ground in relief. "I didn't know you were so good in goal," he cried. "You've stopped all my best shots."

"I'm not sure if that's my goalkeeping or your shooting," Alex laughed.

By half time, Alex had
thrown himself about so much
that he had more dirt on his
kit than any of the players in
the match.

"Look at the state of you!"
his dad exclaimed. "What on
earth have you been doing?"

"Playing in goal," he said
simply. "What's the score?"

"Two each. You should know
that. I told you to watch."

Alex gave a shrug. "Got
bored."

"The manager needs to see
that you're keen," Dad said
grumpily. "Stay close to him in
the second half."

Rafiq was the first sub to join the action. He was sent on when Athletic fell 3–2 behind and he soon supplied the pass for Ben to equalize.

There were just five minutes to go, however, when Alex was called upon, and that was only because of an injury to the left-back. Nobody else was left-footed.

"Just boot it away if the ball comes anywhere near you," the manager told him. "Don't try anything clever."

Alex only had two touches of his ball – and neither of them were very clever.

His first touch was a big hoof
upfield that sailed out of play
for a throw-in.

The second was a deflection
off his knee that skidded past
his own goalkeeper, David, into
the net. An own goal!

There was no time for
Athletic to equalize again.
They lost 4–3.

Alex didn't expect anyone to
speak to him after the game,
but he was wrong. Louis, Ben
and David all had plenty to
say!

Chapter Three
Magic Alex!

"Great save, Alex!" cried Rafiq.

It was the first day of the Christmas holidays and the two boys were playing in the park. They hadn't really known each other very well before that match a fortnight ago, but they were now firm friends.

Alex lay flat out on the ground, as if posing for photographers. He was pretty pleased with the save too.

"I just managed to get my fingertips to it," he said, scrambling back onto his feet to fetch the ball.

"I wish you had been in goal last Sunday," Rafiq called out. "David even let one shot in through his legs."

"Yeah, I know," Alex replied, throwing the ball to him. "I was there, remember."

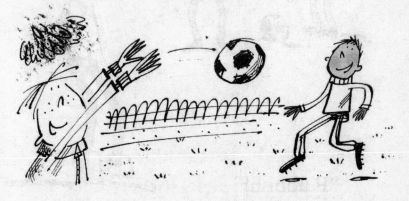

He doubted if anybody else would remember. He hadn't even been given the number thirteen shirt.

"I think David ought to be dropped from the team," said Rafiq, "and then you could—"

"Rubbish!"

Ben's shout startled them.
They had no idea he'd been
behind a tree, spying on their
game.

"Belt up, Raffy!" Ben sneered.
"David's OK. He's just a bit off
form, that's all."

"A *bit* off form!" Rafiq laughed. "Well, I just hope I'm not playing when he's a *lot* off form!"

Ben responded by demanding the ball. "Come on, give it here. I'll show how easy it is to beat Jelly-Belly."

Rafiq flicked the ball up into the air for Ben to volley.

Alex dived to make the save, holding onto the ball with both hands at full stretch.

Ben could hardly believe it. "Huh! Lucky," he muttered. "If I'd hit it right, you wouldn't have smelled it."

"Come off it!" Rafiq scoffed. "He's just saved your best shot."

"Rubbish! Let me have another go."

It took Ben almost ten minutes before he finally put the ball past Alex and even that was from a rebound off the tree trunk.

"So what do you think about Alex's goalkeeping now, eh?" asked Rafiq.

Ben gave a shrug, but the casual gesture was not very convincing. "Well, not bad, I suppose," he admitted.

"Not bad? He's magic!" Rafiq grinned. "He's Magic Alex!"

Chapter Four

In Goal

"Put Jelly-Belly in goal!" scoffed Louis. "You've got to be joking!"

"No, he's OK, honest," said Ben. "I saw him playing in the park yesterday."

The Athletic squad were
having an evening practice
session in the local sports centre
and Louis was not pleased to
find Alex in his team for a
series of five-a-side games.

"Well, I guess it might not be a bad idea," Louis said with a smirk. "He'll fill most of these small goals with his belly!"

Rafiq helped Alex get off to a good start. Rafiq was playing in the opposing team and soon had a clear sight of goal. Alex had faced so many of Rafiq's shots recently that he sensed where his pal was going to place the ball.

It was low to his right, but
Alex didn't even need to dive.
He just made sure he had his
body behind his hands as an
extra line of defence and
gathered the ball up, hugging it
to his chest.

"Good take, J–B," Louis called
out, not wanting to use his
normal nickname for Alex
while Alex's dad was in
earshot. "To me!"

Alex rolled the ball out to his
captain. Louis played a neat
one-two exchange of passes
with Ben to sweep the length
of the short pitch and score at
the other end.

The goal helped to put Louis in a good mood and it set up their team for a winning start. They won their next game too, a much harder contest, mainly due to Alex making a number of fine saves.

"I don't believe it," Louis said as they took a breather while another game was in progress. "Jelly-Belly's kept two clean sheets."

Ben grinned. "David will be getting worried. You know, with all the goals we've been letting in on Sundays."

Their final game was against David's team and the manager watched the two keepers in action with interest.

"I didn't know your lad was any good in goal," he said to Alex's dad.

Dad shook his head. "No, neither did I," he had to admit. "I always have him taking shots at me when we practise together."

Alex made two more good saves,

but he was beaten at last by a shot that flew beyond his reach into the corner of the net.

He didn't mind too much. Ben and Louis had already scored to earn them a 2–1 victory.

"Well done, son – you were great!" Dad praised him as they walked home through the rain. "Come into town with me tomorrow. I want to get you an early Christmas present."

"What's that?" Alex asked excitedly.

"You'll see," Dad grinned. "I believe you have to *look* the part to *play* the part."

Chapter Five
Just Brilliant

"No need to give you this today," said the manager, flinging the torn number thirteen shirt into a corner of the hut. "Not now you've got your own gear."

Alex smiled shyly, thrilled to be named as substitute goalkeeper for Athletic's cup match. He had expected some people to make fun of his new goalie kit, but only David had pulled a face.

Even Louis approved of Alex's multicoloured top. "Smart!" he said. "You'll dazzle the Wanderers if they get too close!"

Their opponents, the Wanderers, had a reputation for being high-scorers and soon lived up to it. Within five minutes of the kick-off, David was beaten twice. After the second goal, he sat in the mud, cradling his right hand in pain.

The ball had bent back his fingers as it sped by into the net.

David had to leave the field because of his injury. What hurt him most, however, was the sight of Alex taking his place in goal.

"Go on, son!" urged Dad when Alex was called onto the pitch by the manager. "Show them what you can do."

Alex was soon in the thick of the action. He had to dive into a muddy puddle to make a save and long black stains covered the patterns on his top.

Now he really felt like a goalkeeper!

"Keeper's ball!" he cried, leaping high to claim a catch and end the next attack on his goal.

"Huh!" grunted one of the Wanderers' strikers. "The way that ball sticks in his gloves, anybody would think it belonged to him!"

He didn't know how right he was. The ball even had Alex's name on it!

As Alex's confidence grew, so did that of the whole team. Athletic began to enjoy more possession and the Wanderers' goalkeeper became much busier.

It was no surprise to anyone when Athletic pulled a goal back just before half time with a header by Ben.

"Only 2–1 down now, lads,"
said the manager during the
break. "You're right back in the
game, thanks to Alex."

"Yeah, great stuff, J-B," said
Louis. "I can't see that lot
getting the ball past you."

The captain's forecast proved correct. Alex's safe handling of the ball kept the Wanderers' attack at bay and his long kicks often caused problems for their defence. They were caught out by one of his mighty boots

upfield, which allowed Rafiq to run clear and score a well-deserved equalizer.

The teams were still level at 2–2 when the referee blew for full time.

Ben slapped Alex on the back as the players left the pitch.

"Now we know what J-B really stands for," he said. "Just brilliant!"

"You'll be in goal again for the replay after Christmas," Louis promised him. "I'll make sure of that."

"What about David?" Alex asked.

"Don't worry," said Louis.
"David's seen what you can do
– we all have. He'll just have
to accept that you're our new
number one goalie!"

The manager even helped
Dad to take down the nets.

"Your lad was our Man of
the Match today," he told him.

Dad had never felt so proud.

Meanwhile, a mud-covered
Alex sat happily on a bench in
the changing hut, holding his
clean football. Louis had
washed all the dirt off it for
him under the tap outside the
hut.

Rafiq
took a bar
of chocolate
from his
coat and offered him a piece.

"No thanks, Raffy," Alex said,
resisting the temptation. "I've
just made a New Year's
Resolution."

"A bit early for that, isn't it?"

"Maybe, but I've decided it's about time I lost some of this weight," he said, patting his tummy. "I've had enough of being called Jelly-Belly."

"So how are you going to do that?" asked Rafiq.

"Well, for a start, I'm going to cut right down on chocs and chips," Alex told him. "It's better to be fit than fat!"

Alex tossed the ball over to his mate and pulled off his muddy goalie top to reveal a white T-shirt with a picture of a goalie printed on the front.

"You know what I'm going to do when I get home, Raffy," he said.

"After you've had a bath, you mean?" Rafiq chuckled.

Alex grinned. "Yeah – and then I'm going to take some of those old footie posters off my bedroom wall to make space for lots of new pictures of goalkeepers!"

"Magic!" Rafiq laughed, flicking the ball back towards Alex. "Catch – keeper's ball!"

THE END